Bootleg Music
and
Other Stories

To Sibyl Severn, whose
writing I admire and admire.
Fondly,

Bob Miles

Bootleg Music
and
Other Stories

Robert W. Miles

SUNSTONE PRESS

SANTA FE

Sunstone books may be purchased for educational, business, or sales promotional use.
For information please write: Special Markets Department, Sunstone Press,
P.O. Box 2321, Santa Fe, New Mexico 87504-2321.

Book and Cover design ▶ Vicki Ahl
Body typeface ▶ Californian FB
Display typeface ▶ Matura MT Script Capitals
Printed on acid free paper

Library of Congress Cataloging-in-Publication Data

Miles, Robert W., 1920-
  Bootleg music and other stories / by Robert W. Miles.
       p. cm.
  ISBN 978-0-86534-832-5 (softcover : alk. paper)
  I. Title.
  PS3613.I53224B66 2011
  813'.6--dc23

                    2011029617

WWW.SUNSTONEPRESS.COM
SUNSTONE PRESS / POST OFFICE BOX 2321 / SANTA FE, NM 87504-2321 /USA
(505) 988-4418 / ORDERS ONLY (800) 243-5644 / FAX (505) 988-1025

Contents

Preface

*W*ritten over a period of several years these stories relate some of the writer's most interesting, provocative, and amusing experiences and express his reactions to them.

Arranged chronologically the stories cover the period 1929 in Lynchburg, Virginia through 1958 in New York City with lengthy sojourns along the way in Lexington, Kentucky; Rome, Georgia; Washington, DC; and Pittsburgh, Pennsylvania.

In each story the unfolding narrative of events predominates; the subjective reactions to and analyses of these events arise naturally from the narrative account. The tone is engaging and conversational. There is an underlying musical rhythm to the prose that carries the reader happily along.

In the first story, "The Athlete" humor is inherent in the reaction of other children to the spectacle of a spindly, underweight boy trying year after year to become a well-functioning athlete. This humor morphs inevitably into pathos at the end of the story due to the fact that this underweight boy, now a teenager, is never allowed to play in an athletic contest.

In "Pancakes" seeing her former philosophy major university class mate trying to function as a short-order cook in a Washington, DC restaurant drives a young woman into screams of uncontrollable laughter. That says it all.

A good example of narrative events provoking reflection, analysis, and speculation is "The Prisoner." In this story the author feels a real need to understand what made him behave the way he did in an Army assignment. His excessive zeal on one occasion was followed by total incompetence as a military policeman on another assignment. The analysis of what made this happen is quite plausible. However the intriguing narrative of the story is still paramount.

The title story, "Bootleg Music" takes place at the Juilliard School of Music in New York City. The writer is using up his G.I. Bill of Rights there after having been discharged from the Army and studying two years at his alma mater, the University of Kentucky. In this story narration outweighs reflection and analysis, and a good deal of this narrative unfolds in dialog.

"Amsterdam Avenue" is a quintessential New York story with the bartender who watches over everyone, the "regulars," and the drunk who is asked to leave and then escorted out. The narrator may appear to the reader to be a little naïve and inexperienced in the ways of the world, but he is also perceptive and learns fast. The narrative element is strong, and the dialog gives the story its New York flavor.

The final story, "The Two Anns," also set in New York shows the narrator to be a songwriter trying to "make it." Though well into his thirties he is still a little uneasy with women. His characteristic determination is much in evidence with the result that this story has both action and suspense.

But there is a happy ending.

The Athlete

When my father died in 1952 some people whom I had not seen in many years came to the house. One of them was the head master of a boy's preparatory school in Georgia. He had been my father's closest friend. With him was the school's athletic director. The two of them were sitting on the sofa in the living room talking, and I kept hearing the phrase, "winning team." That surprised me, not because they weren't talking about my father—people more often than not talk about other things on such occasions. It surprised me because fourteen years earlier, when I had been a student at their prep school, these same men had always said, "It isn't whether you win or lose that matters; it's how you play the game."

When I was nine years old my father had introduced me to athletics by taking me to the YMCA in Lynchburg,

Virginia, where we were living at the time, and signing me on for swimming lessons. He, himself, had been a good athlete in college, and I'm sure he thought it was time to start building me up. I certainly needed it. I was scrawny and spindly and have been told, not unkindly, by two of my aunts that when I was born I looked like a picked chicken. Several childhood illnesses had, I'm afraid, kept me looking something like that; but I liked swimming, and what I lacked in physical endowment I tried to make up for by perseverance. Consequently in about a year's time I was a reasonably good swimmer for my size and took a good deal of pride in that fact.

My father was a minister, and in 1933 he accepted an invitation to become the pastor of the First Presbyterian Church of Lexington, Kentucky. I was thirteen at the time. Shortly after we moved to Lexington my career as a swimmer was almost ended before it had fairly well begun. The Episcopalian bishop of the Diocese of Lexington had made our family feel right at home there from the beginning. One of the nicest things he did was to sponsor our membership in the Lexington Country Club. The bishop had a daughter, Nancy, who was my age. So it was that one day, while the bishop and my father were on the terrace of the club having iced tea, Nancy Abbot, a female friend of hers and I went swimming in the country club pool, located a good distance away on the other side of the club house.

Nancy was somewhat less hospitable than her

father; in fact she and her little friend were teasing me unmercifully. First, they ridiculed the way I looked in my bathing suit. Then, learning that I was leery of the diving platform, they dared me to go up there with them. Once there they pushed me back and forth between them like a medicine ball. What was bound to happen on that narrow platform did. One of them failed to "catch" me, and I went hurtling off the edge, not toward the pool but in the direction of the concrete walk surrounding it. Only by the wildest and most desperate contortions in mid-air— spindly arms and legs flailing madly—was I able to clear the edge of the pool just barely, grazing my left ear and scraping my leg as I did so.

This misadventure, I'm glad to say, didn't stop me from swimming; it just caused me to steer clear of Nancy Abbot and her friend. I spent many hours in that same pool, perfecting my overhand stroke and flutter kick, increasing my speed and duration, developing the capacity to swim under water, and in every way becoming a better swimmer. Nor did I neglect diving. I got so I could do a swan dive or a double flip off that ill-fated platform, cutting the water like a knife, legs and feet perfectly together.

It was in Lexington also that I began to expand my athletic repertory by becoming interested in basketball. My father, glad to see this spontaneous interest in the sport in which he had excelled in college, had a basketball goal installed over the garage doors. The hours I had spent on swimming were few compared to those I now spent trying to learn basketball. Swimming was restricted to the summer months, but I could work on basketball all year, and I remember not a few times, hands so cold I could hardly hold the ball, doggedly practicing shots, sometimes even in the snow.

The next summer the recruiting team from the Georgia preparatory school visited Lexington, and I enrolled there for the fall. In answer to my questions about swimming and basketball I was assured that the athletic program was designed to fit the needs of every student regardless of his ability and experience and that in the best tradition of athletics the emphasis was on physical development through practice and character building through learning how to be a team player.

Late that fall, when the time came to try out for basketball, I knew the varsity team was out of the question. I had neither the height nor the experience for it. However, I did think I would have a good chance of making the junior varsity. The coach, though, took one look at me and said I'd be better off on the midget team. The midget team? The very name was demeaning. I tried out for it and was admitted, but since it seemed to be a repository for everyone who hadn't made the varsity or junior varsity I didn't consider it much of a distinction. Still, I shouldn't have been so lofty about it. A few of us, though on the team, were never allowed to play in a game because the coach didn't think we were capable of helping the team win.

That's fine. But what happened to the idea that winning is not important? It's how you play the game that counts? And what about body building, team playing, and character development? How can you become a team player and develop character if you're not permitted to play? The answer came to me one day as I sat on the bench in the gym watching my teammates in a hard-fought contest. By never being allowed in a game when you have been practicing long, hard, and conscientiously and are all primed and eager to go, you learn to sustain disappointment with equilibrium, and that builds character, doesn't it?

Oh, well, so I wasn't a great basketball player. The swimming team would be formed in the spring, and I would certainly have a good chance of getting on it. After all, I had been swimming longer than playing basketball and was, I knew, better at it.

The tryout for the swimming team was hard, no doubt about it, but I handled myself well. Each applicant had to swim the length of the pool several times as fast as he could. I gave it everything I had, bringing to bear all the practice I had put in at the Lexington Country Club. When it was over the coach took me aside and said I had done very well. He liked my style, my form. I was really a very good swimmer. But unfortunately because of my size I just didn't have the force they would need for a winning team. There it was again, a winning team.

I went back to the dormitory and, because my roommate was there, went into the bathroom, which was empty at that mid-afternoon hour. Leaning over one of the sinks in front of the long row of mirrors I cried my eyes out. I couldn't stop. I must have been there over an hour. The strength of character I had developed from not being allowed to play in the basketball games was not standing me in very good stead. A part of me died that very day. A piece of me broke off and ran down the drain of that sink, disappearing forever.

Pancakes

$\mathcal{E}$very time I enjoy pancakes, I am reminded of an incident in this story. In late 1942 I was stuck in Washington, DC without a cent. I had gotten myself into this predicament in the following way.

I had graduated from the University of Kentucky in June, 1942 with a degree in Philosophy. I took advantage of an opening in the Philosophy Department at Ohio State University in Columbus, Ohio to teach beginning students in summer school preparatory to working on a Masters degree.

But as the summer wore on I was becoming more and more preoccupied with the war, and I kept saying to myself that I should be doing something constructive pertaining to it. Anything but military service, that is. As a freshman at the University of Kentucky I had been kicked off the drill field by a sergeant who yelled, "Miles, there ain't room on this field for you and me, and I ain't leaving!"

However, some kind of government work would certainly contribute more to the war effort than teaching philosophy, wouldn't it? And so when summer school ended, I gave up my position at Ohio State as well as any further thought of getting a Masters degree. With the little money I had managed to put aside I headed straight for Washington, DC.

In Washington I settled into an inexpensive rooming house and started walking the streets from one government office to another. It soon became evident that the last thing anyone in wartime Washington wanted was someone with a background in Philosophy. This realization coincided exactly with my running out of money completely. I was there alone with no one to fall back on. What to do? I literally didn't know where the next meal was coming from.

Yes I did. I would get a job in a restaurant. At that time in the East there was a chain of inexpensive restaurants named Child's. I had been eating most of my meals in one of these near my rooming house. That afternoon I went into that restaurant and let the manager know I would work for a low wage if, in return, I were given my meals free. Being short of applicants in war time he took me on and started breaking me in as a short order cook behind a very long counter running the length of the restaurant.

Of course I didn't tell the manager how new all this

was to me. Back home in Kentucky I had never even made a sandwich or a cup of coffee for myself. The only time I ever went into the kitchen was to ask what I might buy at the corner grocery for our wonderful cook. But here in the Child's Restaurant it didn't take the manager long to learn how little I knew.

The first time a couple came in and ordered pancakes I said to myself I would make them the size I had always wanted when ordering them in a restaurant. As I was pouring the batter onto the immense grill the manager came by and said, "Hey, mister, them cakes look like blankets." Another time, when I was trying to learn how to make coffee in the gigantic urn, I ended up with an inch of scalding water all over the tile floor. This time the manager yelled, "What are you, crazy? You think I'm gonna swim through here?"

Obviously my days at Child's were numbered. One of the last days I was there a girl who had been a class mate of mine at the University of Kentucky came into the restaurant. I assumed she must now be working in a government office. When she saw me behind the counter, her initial surprise gave way to screams of uncontrollable laughter.

Even though, as I remember now, I had worked in the restaurant no more than a week and a half, I had enough money to make my way to nearby Baltimore, where I landed a job in a shipyard as a rigger's helper on the midnight to eight in the morning shift seven days a week. Now I felt that I was really contributing something to the war effort.

But the draft board back in Lexington, Kentucky decided that it was time for me to come back home. So it was that on December 7, 1942—one year to the day after Pearl Harbor—I was inducted into the Army.

The Prisoner

After teaching a year in a junior high school, the chaos in the classroom the last week of school was just as great as it had been the first week ten months earlier. At no time did I master the art of discipline, and I was forced to the reluctant conclusion that you either have the ability to discipline people or you don't, just as you either have an ear for music or you don't. If you don't, no amount of training will help very much. A strong teacher can walk into the classroom and say nothing; his mere presence causes a sepulchral hush to fall over the students. There is "something about him." The teacher without this something can use every rule in the book and every bit of psychological advice offered him, all to no avail.

The good disciplinarian can walk a line between being too easy and too hard. His strength gives him the confidence one must have to treat people in a reasonable way. The poor disciplinarian is unable to walk this line. He starts out by being too permissive, the results of which are disastrous. Then, out of frustration at not being able to teach anything, he develops a false bravura or becomes excessively mean, either of which is unnatural to him. Such a person should be in a line of work more congenial to his nature.

But such freedom of choice is not always possible; certainly it had not been for me twenty-five years earlier during the Second World War. By some inscrutable military logic, I, slight of build and mild of manner, had been made a military policeman and assigned to a detachment in Pittsburgh. Our job was to apprehend every soldier we could find in the western half of Pennsylvania who was away from his camp without leave—AWOL.

Like regular policemen we worked in pairs, some of us riding the train from Pittsburgh to Philadelphia checking all passes to see that no soldier had overstayed his leave, others patrolling the streets and bars. When we found an AWOL soldier we would call headquarters, a truck would be dispatched, and the soldier would be kept under lock and key until an MP from his camp came to take him back.

I suspect that secretly we envied these poor guys who had what seemed to us the courage and enterprise to do what we really wanted to do—run away from camp and go home. Having been strictly brought up, it would have been as hard for me to overstay a pass by five minutes as it was for some of them to go back to camp when they were supposed to. But our very envy of these soldiers caused us to dislike them all the more. This is not to say we should have condoned their behavior, but I think we should have tried to understand it and to have some compassion for them. Yet perhaps we realized that feeling sorry for these soldiers would have been too lacerating day after day. It was easier to grow a calloused exterior and think of them only as AWOLs, not as individuals. Most of them were, in fact, poor individuals, victims of their backgrounds and prey to their own weaknesses. But all too often the roughness of our manner toward them was gratuitous; we treated them more as hardened criminals than fellow soldiers. Admittedly, in some situations such as this it is not easy to do an unpleasant but necessary job and at the same time maintain all the values you think important. But one should at least be aware of it as a problem.

However, just as in the classroom I had never learned to steer a course between the Scylla of being too hard and the Charybdis of being too easy, so neither had I learned to do this in the Army many years earlier. One day in 1944 I was sent with another MP to an address in a poor section of Pittsburgh to see if a missing soldier was with his wife. Right enough, there he was. He seemed almost to be waiting for us, and I thought he appeared relieved, if anything, that we had finally found him. He had come home on a three-day pass and simply stayed on, I am sure as much as a point of honor as out of a spontaneous desire to do so. Now that we were there the dreadful duty to stay away from camp was lifted, and the prospect of being brought back under guard was something he could look forward to because then none of his buddies would be able to say he had chickened out and come back on his own. He had only one request, which was that we leave him alone with his wife for a couple of minutes so he could tell her goodbye.

It was not an unreasonable request, but suddenly, as much to my own surprise as anyone else's, I hit the ceiling. No, he could not say goodbye to his wife alone; he had to go with us that very minute. I knew he wasn't trying to put one over on us and slip out the back door. He even offered to let me hold his wallet as an insurance against any such maneuver. But I would have none of it. How dare he ask us to let him have any more time when he had already been away from camp without leave for so long!

Couldn't I have gotten him back to headquarters expeditiously yet safely and still been decent about it? Was there any justification for following the letter of the law with such obduracy, any reason not to let him have a few final minutes with his wife alone? It began to look as though being a military policeman was bringing out the worst in me: I was envious of the soldier for having the psychological freedom to go AWOL and also for having a wife. And I was spiteful. My zeal was excessive, my punctilio absurd.

The expression on the soldier's face as the other MP and I dragged him unceremoniously off to the truck was an amalgam of bewilderment, contempt, unhappiness, and rage—an expression appropriate to the occasion it must be admitted.

After this episode I brooded about the habit I was slipping into of being gratuitously mean. I resolved that the next time I was sent to pick up an AWOL I would be properly firm and military, yet reasonable and human, but decided also that if I were not strong or mature enough to handle the problem so responsibly, I would from now on rather err on the side of being too nice than not nice enough. I was getting tired of having to kick myself for being brutish.

I didn't have to wait long for the chance to try putting my new resolutions into effect. One Sunday afternoon I was dispatched on the bus to a small town south of Pittsburgh to pick up an AWOL soldier the civilian police had arrested and confined in the county jail. My instructions were to handcuff the prisoner to myself and leave the handcuffs on until I had delivered him safely to the military police barracks back in Pittsburgh.

On the way down I decided against the handcuffs as repugnant and outrageous and vowed I would submit neither the prisoner nor myself to that indignity. If that other AWOL soldier could see me now, I thought, maybe he wouldn't think I was such a bad guy after all.

The soldier I now had to deal with turned out to be even smaller than I, and, although only in his early twenties, he walked with a slight stoop. He had been away from his camp quite a long time and was wearing some rather ratty looking civilian clothes. The first thing he wanted to do when we got outside the jail was take a walk around the block before heading for the bus station. He complained that he had been cooped up in the jail for two days and was badly in need of some fresh air and exercise. Even in my benign state of mind I knew this would be terribly risky. I explained that I was already stretching a point by not putting on the handcuffs and said firmly we were going straight to the bus station.

On the bus he embarked on an harangue that didn't end until we reached Pittsburgh. The burden of this dreary and tedious monologue was that he had one foot in the grave. The physical ailments he told me about with so much relish would have killed any three strong men long ago. I was treated to an account of every asthma attack he had suffered in the past year and a half; I was given a detailed and graphic description of every symptom he had felt just before being rushed to the base hospital in the middle of the night with acute appendicitis; and I was invited to feel a steel plate in his back, placed there after he had sustained some ghastly accident on the firing range.

This avalanche of verbiage had me pinned to the seat with a feeling of intolerable boredom and embarrassment. I was *his* prisoner. Listening to him go on and on I withdrew into myself as an escape, hardly caring by this time that I was thereby impairing my ability to respond adequately to what might happen next.

When we got to the bus station in Pittsburgh the soldier became silent. If I had been functioning properly I might have read this as the ominous sign that it was. I called headquarters to let them know we were back and was told to wait in front of the railroad station across the street for the MP pick-up truck, which would be there right away. Leading up to the railroad station was a very broad sidewalk abutted by a thick stone wall about four feet high. The outer side of the wall was a sheer drop of fifteen feet to the railroad tracks. The sidewalk was so broad it easily accommodated a little Salvation Army canteen trailer hut, a permanent fixture during the war.

As we passed the canteen on our way to the station the soldier clutched his stomach and doubled up with pain. He barely managed to gasp that his ulcer was acting up and begged me to get him a glass of milk. Since whatever resistance to him I had started out with had by now been worn to a nub and since I knew he was going to be taken off my hands any minute, I couldn't see anything wrong with getting him the milk, especially as I didn't have to go into the canteen for it but only ask through the open doorway and have it handed out. But in the few seconds it took to do that this human wreck of an AWOL soldier had vaulted over the wall and jumped the fifteen feet to the tracks below. When I came to and saw what had happened, he was running along the tracks toward the mouth of a tunnel as fast as his asthma, his ulcer, and the steel plate in his back would take him, which was about the speed of an Olympic runner. I was told later by the people who had gathered around that when I saw him running along the tracks, I pulled my revolver out and pointed it in his direction, then apparently thought better of that, put the gun back in my holster, and started running down the sidewalk in the direction of the tunnel exit, presumably with the idea of heading him off at that end.

Just then the MPs I had called drove up. I jumped into the truck and we went racing back to the exit of the tunnel, which was three blocks away. The soldier was nowhere around. Four of us combed the tunnel with flashlights for as long as it took to learn he wasn't hiding in there. The distance from the place he jumped to the entrance of the tunnel was so great I don't see how, regardless of how fast he was running, he could possibly have gotten out the other end and away before we got there; and to this day I wonder what happened to him.

One could say that if I had put the handcuffs on as instructed, it wouldn't have happened. But isn't it a deeper truth that if I had been disposed to handcuff the soldier in the first place, by the same token I wouldn't have had to handcuff him? It harks back to what I said in the beginning.

If I had been a natural disciplinarian with that indefinable air of authority and the consequent ability to do a thankless job with distinction, I would not have fallen into the trap of being too hard on the first AWOL soldier and then, in bending over backward to atone for that, too easy on the second one. And if I had been such a person in the classroom all my students would have fallen silent the minute the bell rang and I walked into the room.

Bootleg Music

J received an honorable discharge from the Army in 1946 and returned to my home in Lexington, Kentucky. There, under the G.I. Bill of Rights I enrolled at my alma mater, the University of Kentucky and began working towards a masters degree in English with the somewhat vague idea of teaching that subject at the university level.

At the same time my great love for music was now manifesting itself in the form of unbidden fragments of original melodies going through my head and insisting on being completed, written down, and shown to others. This entailed music lessons and many hours studying the works of other songwriters. By the time I received the MA in English I had resolved to use what was left of the G.I. Bill of Rights by continuing my study of music.

A wise and experienced Lexingtonian told me that if I

were really serious about studying music full time, I should go to the Juilliard School of Music in New York, both for the quality of the instruction there and for the quality of the music I would get to hear in New York. This advice simply confirmed what I had already suspected. Having really made up my mind months earlier, I made the move in the summer of 1948, giving myself time to get settled in New York and to enroll at Juilliard for the fall semester.

In my first letter to my parents I wrote, "I hope you are reconciled to my studying music and are not disappointed that I am not doing something else. I really need about four lifetimes to do everything." A few days later, having enrolled at the school, I wrote them, "I like the atmosphere at Juilliard very much. It is liberal and stimulating."

One of my favorite classes at the school was Jazz Piano Improvisation, taught by the talented and imaginative John Mehegan. In addition to the informed and instructive criticism by Mehegan we students would listen to each other play and then offer what we hoped was constructive criticism. Mehegan would act as a catalyst and bring all of our comments into meaningful focus.

In a limited sense each of us in this combination class/workshop was a teacher. I found myself enjoying the role and wishing perhaps for a chance to extend myself in it. Fortuitously one of the other members, a Mrs. Barton had come to feel, rightly, that I had been of especial help to her; and when at the end of the semester she asked if I would give her private lessons, I said to myself, "I have a student."

Neither Mrs. Barton nor I would be returning to the class the following semester; I, because the G.I. Bill of Rights had expired. Mrs. Barton, I suppose, because she wanted to study with me.

But she wanted to take these lessons at Juilliard. I pointed out to her that if we were not enrolled we would not be entitled to use the school's facilities. Mrs. Barton brushed this objection aside with a shrug, saying that we could always find an empty practice room for our lessons and that, besides, since we had been students there so recently, who would know that we didn't still belong there?

"But why," I asked, "can't we use your apartment or mine?" "Oh, no," she said, "there wouldn't be any chaperon."

That stopped me dead in my tracks. It was unanswerable on every level. "Besides," she said, "I love the atmosphere at Juilliard. I don't think I would be able to learn anything anywhere else."

"I don't think you'll be able to learn anything anywhere," I said to myself, but cravenly agreed to meet her the next day in the student lounge at Juilliard. I didn't want to lose my first student before I had even got started. Besides, she could be right about Juilliard. I had heard of songwriters, for example, who couldn't write a note unless they were locked in a two-by-four office somewhere with a dinky piano.

The next day, sitting in the student lounge at Juilliard

waiting for Mrs. Barton, I felt neither the comfortable immunity one feels in unfamiliar, new surroundings nor the familiar assurance of a student or faculty member. I felt guilty. But before I had time to change my mind and head for the door Mrs. Barton came in and announced she had arrived before me and had already found an empty class room. "A *class* room, not a *practice* room!" I said to myself, shuddering. I followed her down the hall, feeling as though I were being led to the guillotine.

As it turned out I had nothing to be afraid of. Once or twice someone opened the door and started to come in, but seeing us, backed out apologetically. I began to feel that I really did belong there. And it was such a lovely place in which to give lessons—the room was light, airy, soundproofed, and equipped with a Steinway grand piano. My career as a music teacher, legitimate or not, was getting off to an impressive start.

It is remarkable and unsettling how short a time it takes the mind to justify wrong-doing. By the time I went up to Juilliard the next week I had managed to forget that I didn't belong there, so that when Mrs. Barton and I couldn't find an empty room right away, I became irritated. Those students practicing had no right to deprive us of a place for our lessons. Mrs. Barton, on the other hand, had no mental adjusting to do. She had never for a minute felt that she should take her lessons with me anywhere but at Juilliard.

But she and I were in for some rough sledding now. This semester there was a great run on practice rooms. Some days we would have to cover almost the whole building before finding a vacant room. In order to save time we would split up. Mrs. Barton would start at one end of a corridor and I at the other and we would work our way toward the middle, listening at each door or cracking it just a little. What we heard from within was usually some terribly impressive concerto-sounding passage, which made the business of our lessons—simple jazz chords and halting renditions—seem unimportant indeed.

My recently acquired bravado was becoming seriously undermined. Sometimes, hearing nothing through the door, I would start to walk in, only to find three or four people studying a score or a class room filled with students copying something off the black board. One day I walked into a class that was waiting for a substitute professor whom they didn't know. While I was backing out, explaining that I wasn't their man, I bumped into that gentleman, who was hurrying in head down. His books and papers spilled all over the floor. I retreated in total confusion and escorted Mrs. Barton to the floor above. There I let her do the room-shopping while I stood trembling at the end of the hall under the stairs.

The following week when I went up to Juilliard to meet Mrs. Barton for her lesson, I found inside the front entrance a table with two rosters on it and a guard presiding over them.

"Oh," I said to myself, "he's there because of us."

"Is it necessary to sign in?" I asked the guard.

"Yes," he said. "That's the rule now."

"You haven't been having any trouble, have you?" I asked, noticing a croaking sound in my voice.

"Yes, we have," he said without elaborating. However he let me in when I explained that I was just going to meet a friend in the lounge and wouldn't be long. A few minutes later Mrs. Barton joined me.

"Well," I said, "I guess we really will have to make other arrangements now."

"Oh, don't worry," she said. "The man said we can use a room."

"But what did you tell him?" I asked.

"Never you mind," said Mrs. Barton. "We women have our little ways of doing things."

I let it go at that. That day we had an unusually long lesson, during which I felt even more embarrassed than usual, feeling that we were taking advantage of the guard's good nature in letting us stay there at all. All I wanted was to get out of there fast and unobtrusively and never come back. But when we reached the lobby this impulse was arrested by the guard's hand on my shoulder. I must have jumped a foot.

"Oh, Mr. Miles," he said, unexpectedly calling me by my name. "I'm sorry for stopping you a while ago. If I had known you were Mr. Mehegan's assistant I wouldn't have had you sign in. You won't have to again."

Outside I regained my composure enough to congratulate Mrs. Barton on her presence of mind. "I would never have thought of telling him that," I said. The implications of what she had done hadn't sunk in yet.

Two mornings later the telephone woke me and a voice I didn't recognize at first said, "How's my assistant this morning?"

"Oh, Mr. Mehegan," I said. "I can explain everything—I think."

"You don't have to," he said. "I know Mrs. Barton. But I want you to tell her that if she ever uses my name again without my permission, I'll bring her before the Juilliard authorities."

When I relayed this message by phone to Mrs. Barton, she was abashed.

"Why I had no idea Mr. Mehegan would take an attitude like that," she said. There was a pause, after which she said, "Of course I want to go on taking lessons." Another pause. "I won't be able to for the next two weeks because some relatives from out of town are coming, but as soon as they have left I'll call you."

I'm still waiting.

Amsterdam Avenue

*W*hile living alone and unattached on the Upper West Side of Manhattan in New York City there was a period when I would go into a certain bar on Amsterdam Avenue every night to ease my seemingly chronic tension and anxiety by having a couple of drinks. Of course what would have been even more efficacious in this regard would have been to pick up a girl there. I had been reading magazine articles about the "sexual revolution." Maybe this bar would turn out to be one of the places where it was happening.

Sitting there I would fantasize about old movies in which the leading character would go into a bar and hitch himself up into the best seat, which would always be empty. The bar tender would be deferential and call him "sir." "Will it be the usual tonight, sir?" On the bar stool next to him would be a good-looking and understanding woman like Ida Lupino. He and she would fall naturally into an easy conversation, and that would be the beginning of everything.

But how could the sexual revolution be taking place in this Amsterdam Avenue bar where the bar tender was like a father watching over everybody, especially the women, to see that nobody like me "got fresh" or tried to "start anything"? I was pretty sure that some of the women went to this bar with the same idea as I, but I could just hear their cries of outraged innocence and the bar tender's "Listen, buddy, this ain't that kind of place" the minute I made even the most tentative approach to any of them. Still, what could I do but try?

Tonight the horseshoe-shaped bar was almost filled, but there was still an empty bar stool just as in the movies, and though the girl in the next seat to it wasn't Ida Lupino, it was a girl. I hitched myself up to the bar and ordered a bourbon and water. The girl next to me was a little plump, but she had a nice figure and the kind of straight, casual hair I liked. She was getting drunk on shots of gin and beer chasers.

All the other people in the bar were men except for a platinum blonde at the corner of the bar across from me. She was with a man. The girl next to me getting drunk was talking to herself but also to the room at large. Sometimes she would look in someone's direction as she talked and so in a sense would be talking to them. But she didn't really expect a reply.

Some of the things she said were funny, causing everyone to laugh. But then they would belie the fellowship suggested by the laugh by talking about her in low voices and occasionally looking her way with a kind of contempt.

I wanted to get into a conversation with the girl but was afraid to because of what all the others, especially the bar tender, would think. I had a giddy impulse to slip her a note saying I would meet her in the bar down the street, but then I realized this might strike *her* as a huge joke, which she would then broadcast to the whole bar. So I just ordered my second drink and waited to see what would happen.

The girl started abusing the bar tender because he wouldn't give her another drink. Then she started needling the platinum blonde across the way. "Your hair looks dark at the roots, dear. What you need is a good hair dresser."

"Are you one?" asked the blonde.

"I'm one," said the girl and swung around the other way.

"Okay, let's drink up and go," said the bar tender.

"I'm not drunk," said the girl.

She turned around again and fixed the platinum blonde with a drunken but perceptive stare.

"You look scared, dear," she said. "You're having

a good time and you're getting paid for it, but you look scared. I wouldn't be scared if it was me."

The blonde stared straight ahead into space.

"Come out on the sidewalk with me and I'll show you what it is to be scared," said the drunk girl loudly.

The bar tender came out from inside the horseshoe bar and started escorting her to the door.

"I dare you to come out on the sidewalk with me, you whore," she screamed back over her shoulder.

After she was safely out the platinum blonde said, "What is she, crazy? I didn't say a word to her. Did I say anything to her?"

"You know what's the matter with her?" asked the bar tender rhetorically, leaning over the bar and including as many people as he could in his revelation. "She ain't bar broke."

I was afraid to leave now because they all might think I was going out after the girl who had just been escorted out. So I ordered still another drink. The bar tender handed me the drink and pushed my money back; this one was on the house. Suddenly I felt grateful and warm inside. I belonged. And wasn't that the most important thing after all? To belong?

The Two Anns

One day in 1958 I received a letter from my sister in Japan, where her husband, an Army Major, was stationed, telling me about a friend of hers, Ann, who was separating from her husband, also an Army officer, and returning to New York.

My sister wasn't trying to "fix me up" with a woman, though I was unattached and in my early thirties. But I was a songwriter trying to break into the theater, and Ann's soon-to-be ex-husband was, when not in uniform, a theatrical producer. My sister thought the connection might conceivably help me, despite their estrangement. She explained the breakup to me by saying Ann had "been cutting a wide swath too close to the flag pole." My sister had a way with words.

Ann turned out to be a good looking blonde woman

in her late twenties, a very nice person, engaging and intelligent. I had made a reservation for us in a restaurant on the second floor of an elegant looking brownstone house on East 55th Street, a place I had passed many times because I was giving piano lessons to a friend, also named Anne, who lived on the second floor of the brownstone house right next door. The restaurant had always looked to me as though it held the promise of comfort, relaxation, and good food.

Over dinner Ann and I talked about my sister and brother-in-law, Ann's life as an Army wife—tedious—my life in New York—a struggle, but one I liked. We talked about my music, and Ann said she would like to hear some of it. The restaurant was even cozier than I had expected, and, having had two drinks before dinner and wine with it, Ann and I were enjoying ourselves very much and feeling quite friendly.

"Marian didn't tell me her brother was charming," said Ann.

Though I was over thirty and had had several love affairs (or what used to be called "affairs") I was still shy with women and was always trying to overcome it. So, although Ann's compliment made me feel good, it was also disquieting. But maybe this would be the night I could get over this nonsensical timidity.

So out of bravado, but also out of politeness and because I wanted one, I asked Ann if she would like an after-dinner drink. It was bravado for two reasons: one, because I imagined it would move us closer to the liaison I was feeling two ways about—attracted to but afraid of—and two, because the sickening realization that I didn't have quite enough money to pay for all this was beginning to work its way up. This gorgeous restaurant with its relaxed living ambiance and superb food was just as expensive as it should have been but more expensive than I had thought it would be.

Ann said yes she would love an after-dinner drink and that we should make it a Strega. I had seen advertisements for this liquor, conveying the message not very subtly that it was a stimulant to the libido. But rather than leering at Ann knowingly, which I wasn't good at, I pretended not to know anything about it.

"It's an aphrodisiac!" said Ann, looking me straight in the eye. This, of course, had the effect of making me more anxious, but "great," I said, "let's have one by all means."

But what about the check? Now that things looked so promising it seemed to me what had to be avoided at all costs was the humiliation that would result from telling Ann I didn't have quite enough money after all and could she help out a little.

As I sat there, somewhat mellow and bemused by now, a plan I would never have thought of if completely sober, much less dared to undertake, was beginning to take shape in my mind. It was perfect in its simplicity but would depend on split second timing and a lot of luck. I would just excuse myself to go to the men's room, and the second I was out of sight dash next door and borrow ten dollars from the Anne I gave piano lessons to. The whole plan, of course, depended on that Anne being home, and, if home, having the money to lend me. The waiter brought the Stregas. This Ann and I clinked glasses and took a sip.

"It's really smooth," I said. "I like it a lot." After a momentary pause, "Would you excuse me a minute? I'll be right back."

Was Ann looking at me quizzically, maybe with a little amusement? I now think so, but why should she have been? I was only going to the men's room.

I got up, probably a little unsteadily, and made my way out into the hall. The instant I was out of sight of the people in the restaurant I bolted down the stairs, out on to the sidewalk and into the area way of the brownstone next door.

"Be home, Anne. You've got to be home," I muttered as I pressed the bell. "What am I going to do if you're not?"

But she was. When the buzzer sounded, I raced up the stairs two at a time and practically fell against the door of her apartment.

"I can't come in," I gasped when she opened the door. "I'm in the restaurant next door with a date, and like an idiot I don't have quite enough for the check. Can you lend me ten dollars?"

"Oh, dear, Bobby," she said. "I hope so. Hold on just a second."

"Are you sure you can spare it?" I asked falsely when she came back with the money. "I'll give it back to you Wednesday or you can just not pay for your piano lesson. I'll explain everything then." I literally snatched the bill from her hand and lurched toward the landing.

I sped back down her stairs and up the stairs of the restaurant, stopped long enough to adjust my tie and then walked nonchalantly back into the dining room. I couldn't have been gone more than six minutes. I called for the check and paid the waiter, now able to give him a reasonably good tip.

As I floated down the carpeted stairs of the restaurant with one Ann, I was silently thanking the other one.

This book of short stories has been printed on acid-free paper.

The typeface is Californian FB.

In 1938, Goudy designed California Oldstyle, his most distinguished type,
for University of California Press.

In 1958, Lanston issued it as Californian.

Carol Twombly digitized the roman 30 years later for California;
David Berlow revised it for Font Bureau with italic and small caps;
Jane Patterson designed the bold.
In 1999, assisted by Richard Lipton & Jill Pichotta,
Berlow designed the black and the text and display series.

CPSIA information can be obtained at www.ICGtesting.com
Printed in the USA
LVOW062039170911

246734LV00002B/7/P